The story of
Marlu
The Mango Lunchkin

SS Ravula • P Narayanan

About the Author: SS Ravula
Author, Entrepreneur, Physician, but mostly a Mom and sometimes a very passable Cook.

About the Illustrator: P Narayanan
Artist, Geek, Dreamer. All three. All the time!

Please support our vision and mission toward bringing nutritiously delicious lunched made from Organic, All-natural, non-GMO ingredients and daily servings of fruits and vegetables to school children.

Please visit www.lunchkins.com

To order additional copies of this book, contact:
Xlibris
1-888-795-4274
www.Xlibris.com
Orders@Xlibris.com

To

Om, Amiya, Chetan and
the little kid whose imagination is his true flight!

It was a beautiful spring day. All the Lunchkins were on Cove Farm. They were there to celebrate the beginning of the spring planting season.

1

While the adult Lunchkins were busy tilling the soil for crops such as corn, carrots, and potatoes, the little Lunchkins were out in the meadow adjacent to the farm—flying kites, playing tag, and running around with the baby sheep and the farm puppies.

2

Marlu the little Mango Lunchkin, however, was sitting under a tree forlornly watching his friends Bolu, the little Blueberry Lunchkin, and Carlu, the little Carrot Lunchkin, flying a green kite with its long tail furling in the breeze against the bright blue sky.

"Hey, Marlu why the long face?" asked Mommy Mango Lunchkin.

"Nothing," said Marlu in a quiet voice.

"Why aren't you playing with Bolu and Carlu?" asked Mommy Mango Lunchkin, sitting next to him on the soft, thick grass.

"**Well,** they think I'm too little. They say that I cannot run fast enough. They don't want to play with me," confessed Marlu as big fat tears welled in his baby eyes, threatening to spill down his chubby golden cheeks in a hurry.

"**Oh,** Marlu," sighed Mommy Mango Lunchkin while snuggling up to him. "Every Lunchkin is unique in their own special way. So are you. Just give Bolu and Carlu time. You are still little. In time, they will come to realize that you are a true friend and will value you for who you are."

Daddy mango Lunchkin, who had just taken a break from the farm and had been walking up to them, overheard the whole conversation.

"**Come on,** Marlu" he said briskly. "Farmer Kindale has a bunch of kites sitting by the barn. I spotted a red one that I think we can borrow. Would you like to fly one with me?"

"**Yes, yes!**" cried Marlu excitedly, and he ran down the hill with his dad.

A few days later, Marlu and his mom were out in their home garden, picking fresh herbs to season the KuTrient and KeLement soup. Mommy Mango Lunchkin was famous in all of Cove Meadows for her secret KuTrient and KeLement soup. She made this once a week and was very generous in sharing it with all her neighbors.

"**Mommy,** am I getting big now?" asked Marlu.

"**You** are growing up a little each day, Marlu. And even though I miss you from when you were a tiny baby Lunchkin, I am so proud of you with each passing day. You are good and kind. Soon you will notice that you have a very special magic in you."

"**What** is it, Mommy?" eagerly asked a thrilled Marlu.

"**Wait** and see" was all she said.

Summer was soon upon them. Sheep were sheared. Yarn was spun. Spring calves jostled each other desperately trying to prove who was getting bigger faster. The Lunchkins harvested fresh strawberries. They made preserves, jams, and jellies. The cornfields shone brilliantly in the bright summer sun, making Farmer Kindale's heart swell with joy. It was turning out to be quite a busy year for the Lunchkins.

Before they knew it, the Fall Harvest Festival was in full swing. The leaves had turned orange. The breeze was nippy, but the sun was still quite generous with her warmth.

Mommy and Daddy Mango Lunchkin were excited to see the full harvest of apples and grapes. Mommy Mango Lunchkin could almost smell the aroma of freshly baked apple pies that would waft out from Farmer Kindale's kitchen

Marlu skipped along behind his parents hoping that he would run into Bolu and Carlu. Sure enough, they were in the meadow playing tag.

"Hi!" shouted Marlu excitedly. "Can I play tag with you?"

"I don't think so Marlu," said Carlu haughtily. "You are still so little. See, we don't want to see you trip and hurt yourself."

"Well, maybe we could play another game that Marlu can join in," said Bolu kindly. Marlu looked expectantly at Carlu.

"**We'll** see. Come on, Bolu. Let's go fly kites. I've been looking forward to this a long time!" shouted Carlu and he ran toward the barn without glancing back at Marlu. Bolu shrugged his shoulders and ran after Carlu.

Marlu walked to the pond at the bottom of the meadow and watched the ducks swimming around eagerly for the cracked corn being tossed to them by the other little Lunchkins. The drakes were getting bigger and stronger, and quite bold too.

Marlu thought about summer and how badly he wished he had friends. But somehow, he felt different than he did in spring. He didn't feel so sad. He was doing well in school. His parents loved him. And based on what Mommy Mango Lunchkin had told him, it was just a matter of time before his special magic would be revealed to him.

He breathed in the crisp autumn air and started walking toward his favorite tree with a lift in his heart and a leap in his step.

"Hey, catch it, catch it. There it goes!" he heard.

He looked toward the shouts from the meadow. It was Carlu and Bolu chasing their precious green kite. It broke free and was being carried swiftly by the breeze.

Oh, no! Carlu and Bolu will be so sad if they lose it, thought Marlu to himself.

He started running toward the kite. His heart was filled with kindness and love for his friends. He ran faster than he had ever run in his little life. Faster and faster, stronger and swifter. Soon he was running so fast he almost felt like the ground was moving away from him. His heart beat rapidly, and he almost panicked when he realized he was actually moving higher and higher in the air.

With an excited little lump in his throat, he croaked, "I can fly."

He swirled and twirled and leapt and zoomed while all the other little Lunchkins screamed and waved to each other. They had never seen anything so amazing.

Mommy Mango Lunchkin beamed proudly.

Marlu was so excited he almost forgot about the kite. When he realized what he had originally set out to do, he scanned around and found the green kite stuck at the topmost branch of his favorite tree. He zoomed out to it, untangled it, and hurried back to his friends. In his eagerness, he forgot that this was his first flight, and he didn't exactly know how to land. With a bump and a thump, he tumbled down the hill.

He landed with a plonk at Farmer Kindale's feet who had rushed out to see what the commotion was all about.

Marlu looked up sheepishly and then recovered himself while Daddy Mango Lunchkin rushed over and checked his knees and elbows. He slowly realized that everyone was staring at him. But he had eyes only for the green kite. It was torn to shreds after being caught in some bushes.

"**Oh, no,**" cried Marlu, the sadness at the sight of the poor kite overwhelming the joy he had felt at flying. Carlu and Bolu were standing by, staring silently at Marlu and the green kite.

"**I'm sorry.**" Marlu sobbed. "I have ruined your kite."

"**No,** actually you have shown us what a true friend you are!" said Carlu in a soft, kind voice.

"**Please** forgive us for not seeing you for who you are before."

35

Marlu stopped crying and looked up at his mommy. She nodded her head and smiled. Slowly Marlu started smiling too.

All the little Lunchkins started clapping and jumping excitedly.

Carlu and Bolu hugged Marlu tightly and said, "Friends forever!"

Carlu said, "Hey, want to check out how big the spring piglets have grown?"

"**Sure!**" cried Marlu excitedly. "I'd love to. It is fun having friends to do things together!"

"**Plus,** it never hurts to have a flying Mango Lunchkin to help us win a game of piñata." Bolu winked.

The three friends laughed happily while they ran toward the Cove Farm Pen.

How do you "**Mango**"
(get it? Tango Mango)
Known as the King of Fruits, the Mango has been around for over **4000** years!

During this time the Mango has been talked about by the Poet **Amir Khusrao**, the writer **Hsiun Tsang**, travelled with **Alexander the Great**, brought to the people by Emperor **Shah Jahan** and even played a role in the Chinese Cultural Revolution.

Although they primarily grow in **South East Asia**, mangoes are eaten all over the world.
In fact, even though **50%** of the mangoes produced in the world are from **India**, Indians eat most of them!

While the fruit can be eaten raw or ripe, the tree seems to have some interesting side effects on people! **Goddess Ambika** and **Buddha** were both found spending a lot of quality time in the shade of a Mango tree getting strong and wise.

So, what can a Mango do for you? Eating a mango can :

Improve your Vision
Vitamin A

Help aid Digestion
Enzymes

Improve your Memory
Vitamin B6

Attain perfect Skin- **Collagen, Vitamin A, Vitamin C** (Anti-aging and treating Acne)
Treat Anemia-**Iron**
Prevent Cancer- **Pectin**
Help Weight Gain- **Calories**
Help Boost immunity- **Beta Carotene**
Plus its sweet, delicious pulp is loved by millions all over the world.
You can eat it in **salads, salsas, pickles, murabbas, chutneys, museli, sorbets** and even make lots of delicious drinks like **Milkshakes, Aguas frescas, Aam Ras** and **Lassi**!
One can even eat it with fish sauce! (**patis**)
However, be cautious, the sap from the tree, stem and leaves can cause intense itching and rashes.
Is it any wonder that it takes 6 months for a mango to ripen but one can eat it in under 6 minutes!
No wonder nothing says be my friend like a basket of full of ripe delicious Mangoes.

Printed in the United States
By Bookmasters